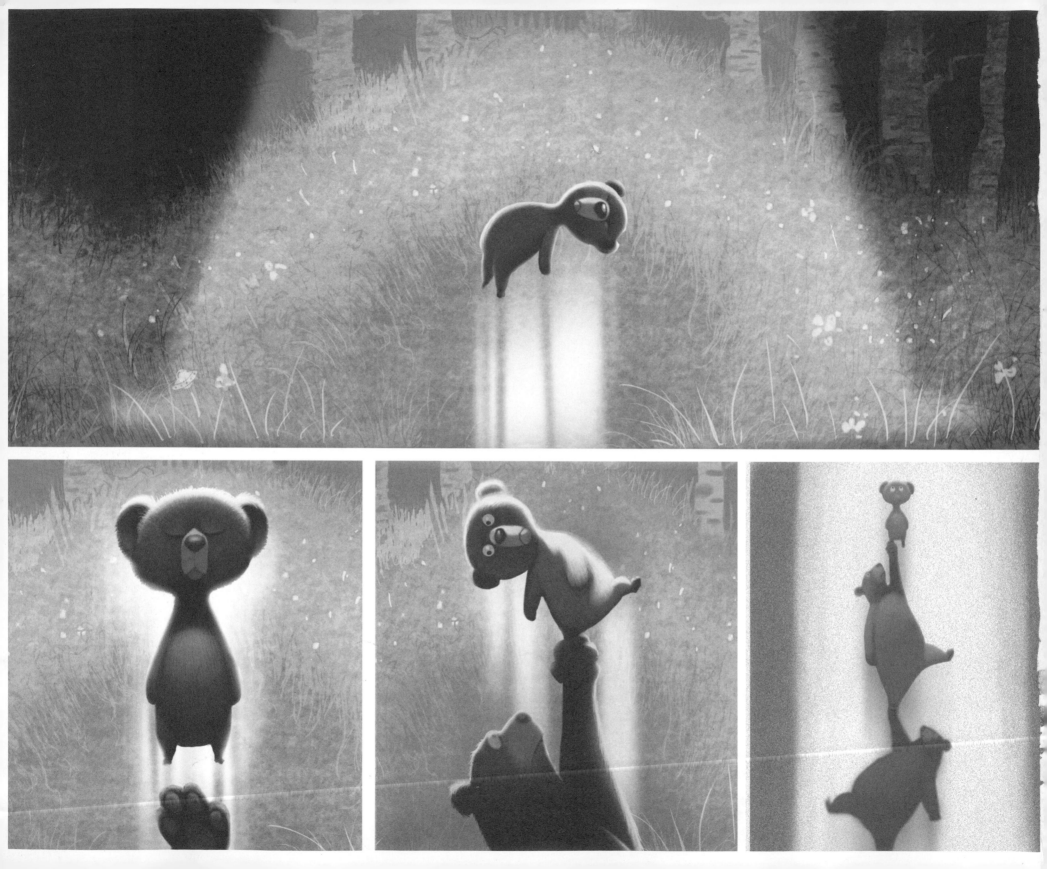

Published by Charlesbridge
85 Main Street
Watertown, MA 02472
(617) 926-0329
www.charlesbridge.com

Library of Congress Cataloging-in-Publication Data
Names: Biedrzycki, David, author, illustrator.
Title: Breaking news : alien alert / David Biedrzycki.
Other titles: Alien alert
Description: Watertown, MA : Charlesbridge, [2018] | Summary: In this story, told in the
form of a television broadcast, the bear family and other forest and domestic animals are
abducted by an alien spaceship, releasing a worldwide media frenzy.
Identifiers: LCCN 2017003929 (print) | LCCN 2017006561 (ebook) | ISBN 9781580898041
(reinforced for library use) | ISBN 9781632896452 (ebook) | ISBN 9781632896469 (ebook pdf)
Subjects: LCSH: Bears—Juvenile fiction. | Animals—Juvenile fiction. | Television broadcasting—
Juvenile fiction. | Alien abduction—Juvenile fiction. | Extraterrestrial beings—Juvenile fiction. |
CYAC: Bears—Fiction. | Animals—Fiction. | Television broadcasting—Fiction. | Extraterrestrial
beings—Fiction. | Humorous stories. | LCGFT: Humorous fiction.
Classification: LCC PZ7.B4745 Bp 2018 (print) | LCC PZ7.B4745 (ebook) | DDC
   [E]—dc23
LC record available at https://lccn.loc.gov/2017003929

Printed in China
(hc) 10 9 8 7 6 5 4 3 2 1

Illustrations done in Adobe Photoshop
Display type set in The Sans by Luc as de Groot
Text type set in Stripwriter by Typotheticals
Color separations by KHL Chroma Graphics, Singapore
Printed by 1010 Printing Limited in Huizhou, Guangdong, China
Production supervision by Brian G. Walker
Designed by Diane M. Earley

At the time of publication, all URLs
printed in this book were accurate and
active. Charlesbridge and the author
are not responsible for the content
or accessibility of any website.

To my wife, Kathy, and Cassandra Sheets
for their awesome contributions

NOW FOR A NEWS 3 SPECIAL REPORT. WE GO TO CHAD NEWSWORTHY, REPORTING LIVE FROM HUNDRED ACRE PARK.
3 NEWS
SPECIAL REPORT

BREAKING NEWS

ALIEN ALERT

Reported by
David Biedrzycki

iↄi Charlesbridge

RIGHT NOW, LET'S GO TO A LIVE PRESS CONFERENCE WITH MAYOR LUKE ATME.
GOOD AFTERNOON, MY FELLOW CITIZENS! I'M NOT HERE TO TALK ABOUT MY ELECTION CAMPAIGN, BUT TO EXPRESS MY DEEPEST CONCERN FOR THOSE POOR, DEFENSELESS ANIMALS.
BREAKING NEWS POLLS SHOW IF ELECTION WERE HELD

POLICE HAVE ROPED OFF THE MEADOW, BUT THAT HASN'T PREVENTED FOLKS FROM STOPPING BY AND TAKING A LOOK.
ALIEN ALERT
NEXT UP: CAN ALIENS READ OUR MINDS?

Meanwhile . . .

REPORTERS FROM ALL OVER THE WORLD HAVE GATHERED HERE TONIGHT. ONE THOUGHT IS ON EVERYONE'S MIND: WE ARE NOT ALONE.
NO ESTAMOS SOLOS.
NIE JESTEŚMY SAMI.
BREAKING NEWS WORLD LEADERS FINALLY AGREE ON

BREAKING NEWS AIR TRAFFIC CONTROL REPORTS LARGE

UNIDENTIFIED FLYING OBJECT ABOVE PARK.

BREAKING NEWS ALIEN SPACESHIP HAS LANDED.

BREAKING NEWS ANIMALS SAFELY RETURN TO EARTH

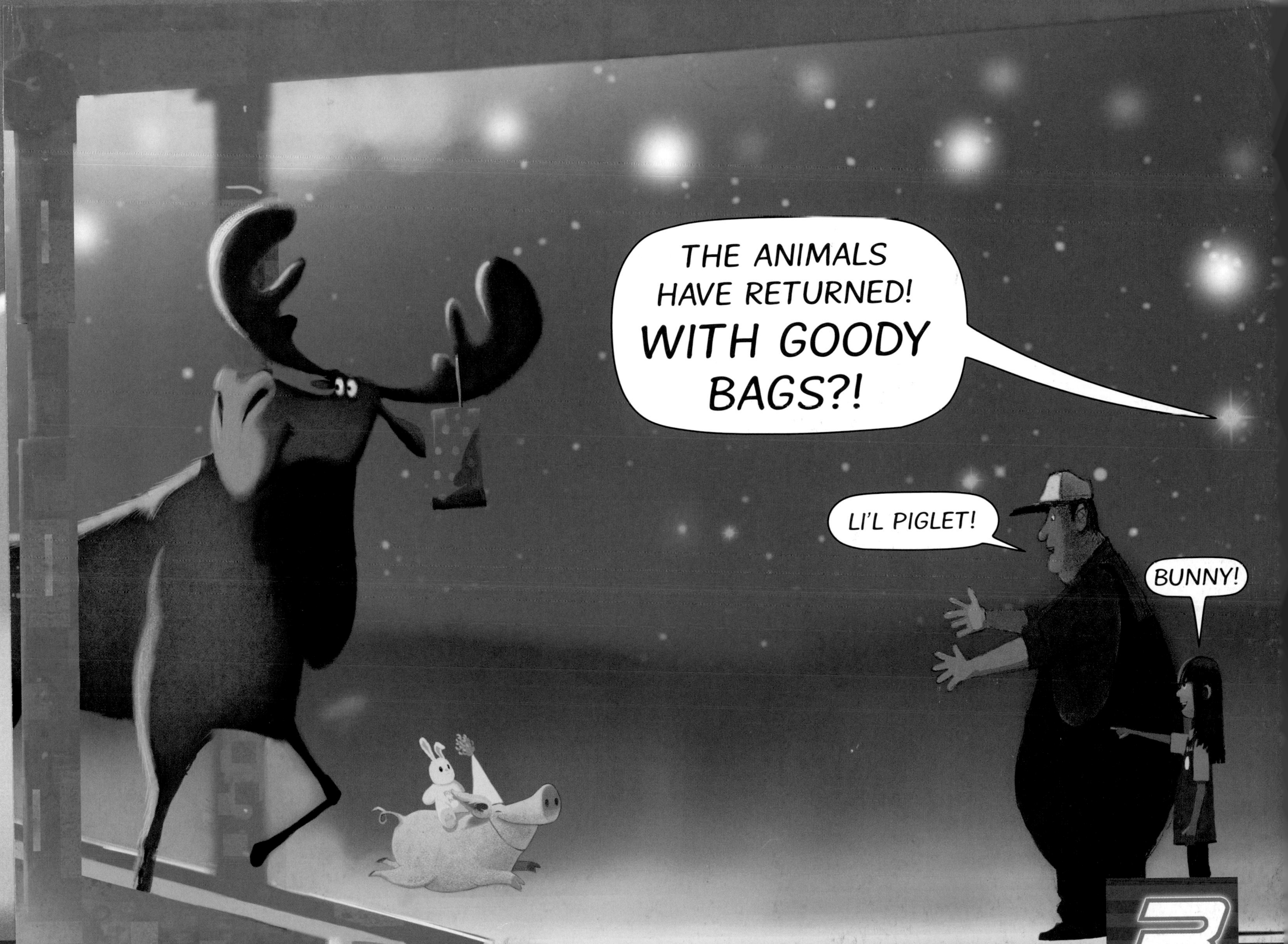

AFTER AN OUT-OF-THIS-WORLD PARTY.